Based on the TV series *Rugrats*® created by Arlene Klasky, Gabor Csupo, and Paul Germain as seen on NICKELODEON®

SIMON SPOTLIGHT
An imprint of Simon & Schuster
Children's Publishing Division
1230 Avenue of the Americas
New York, NY 10020

GROLIER
B O O K S

This edition published by Grolier Books.
Grolier Books is a division of Grolier Enterprises, Inc.

ISBN 0-7172-8977-X

Space Invaders!

By Sarah Albee
Illustrated by Ron Zalme

Simon Spotlight/Nickelodeon

"Tommy, they're after us!" cried Chuckie. He ducked under a pillow.

"Aw, it's just the TV, Chuckie," said Tommy. "The space invaders are not really coming to get us."

"Watch out," said a space creature on TV. "YOU might be NEXT! Ha! Ha! Ha! Ha! Haaaaaaa!"

Chuckie jumped off the couch. He hid behind a curtain. "They'll be here any minute!" he said.

Suddenly, Chuckie saw something out the window. "Uh-oh . . ." he said.

"What, Chuckie?" asked Tommy.

Chuckie pointed. A big scary thing with three legs stood in the backyard.

Chuckie wailed, "We're doomed! The space invaders are here!"

"We won't let them take anyone!" Tommy said bravely.

"*We?*" asked Chuckie in a worried voice.

Just then, Chaz walked into the room. "Thanks for watching Chuckie, Didi," he called. "I hope there's space at the craft show."

Chaz gave his son a hug. "See ya later, Chuckie!" he said.

Chuckie looked at Tommy. "My dad's getting a spacecraft!" he groaned.

Suddenly, they heard loud clanking noises. It was Stu, coming up the stairs. He looked strange.

"Hey kids," said Stu. "It's almost finished! When they get here, I'll be ready!"

Stu peeked out the window. Then he smiled and patted Tommy's head. "I think they're going to like it, Tommy!" he said.

Stu stomped back downstairs.

"They know too, Tommy," Chuckie said. "They're going away with the space invaders!"

Didi stepped out of the bathroom.
"Are you boys playing nicely?" she asked.
"There's so much to do before they get here!"

Tommy and Chuckie looked at her and gasped.

Just then, the phone rang. "Oh, hi, Lucy," said Didi. "Yes, there will be plenty of space for everybody!"

She hung up the phone. "They will be here soon! Lots and lots of them!"

Clack, clack, clack!

Chuckie grabbed Tommy. "Is it them?" he whispered.

But it was just Grandpa Lou dancing down the stairs.

"I can't be late for my old-timer's disco!" he said excitedly. "We're going to moonwalk today! But I'll be back in time. I wouldn't miss it for the world! See ya, sports!"

Then he danced out the door.

"We hafta do something, Tommy," Chuckie said.

"Don't worry, Chuckie," said Tommy. "I'll think of something."

Suddenly, Betty barged in with Phil
and Lil. She put all the babies into the
playpen. "Nice shirt, Chuckie," she said.
"It's perfect for later!"

"Oh, no," Chuckie whimpered.

"Well, time for my marching orders!"
Betty added, before going into the kitchen.

"Martian orders! Did you hear that?" said Chuckie. "Phil, Lil, your mom is becoming a Martian!"

"Why?"asked Phil.

"'Cause the space invaders are gonna take them all away!" Chuckie cried.

The babies were so busy worrying, they didn't notice Stu carrying something out to the backyard.

A little later, Spike trotted in. He had something in his mouth.

"Look! Spike has a space helmet!" cried Tommy. "Spike must've had a fight with the space invader and taken his helmet!"

Tommy quickly opened the playpen. The babies hurried to the window. They thought they would see the space invader lying on the grass. But they saw something else.

"Another space invader!" Chuckie
squeaked.

Sure enough, some other strange thing
was in the backyard. It had blinking lights.
It had bouncy springs. Little puffs of
smoke came out of its head.

"We have no choice," said Tommy. "We have to talk to the space invaders."

"What are you going to tell them, Tommy?" asked Lil.

"I'll tell them they can't have our moms and dads," said Tommy. Then he spoke slowly through the open door. "Attention, please! We are friendly earthlings. Please don't take away our moms and dads!"

Peep-peep! went the space invader.

Woosh-woosh.

Click-click.

"It's TALKING to us!" yelled Lil.

SPLICK!

Something red squirted out from it, right at the babies.

"It's FIRING at us!" yelled Phil.

"We're doomed, doomed, doomed!" wailed Chuckie.

"Waaaah!" yelled the babies. Stu, Didi, and Betty rushed to see what was wrong— just as the doorbell rang.

"It's THEM!" cried Chuckie.

The babies wailed again, "WAAAAAH!"

Stu picked up Tommy. "Gee, I wonder what's bothering the kids?" he said. "Maybe they want to see what's outside. I think they're gonna be blown away!"

"WAAAAAHHH!" yelled the babies, even louder than before.

Everyone trooped outside. All the babies had their eyes closed.

"Look, Tommy," said Stu. Tommy opened one eye. He saw Stu pointing to the space invader.

"Here's the friendly ketchup, mustard, and relish machine!" Stu said proudly. "Nifty, huh?"

The babies looked at one another.

SPLICK! went the machine. Ketchup squirted all over Stu and Tommy.

"Okay, so I have to work out a few kinks," said Stu.

Tommy laughed. So did Chuckie, Phil, and Lil.

Soon everyone was in the backyard.

"Great day for a barbecue, Didi," said Mr. Carmichael. "And that's uh, a very interesting invention, Stu." Mr. Carmichael looked down at the blob of ketchup on his shirt.

"Thanks!" said Stu.

"Yep. These are great hot dogs, Deed," said Betty. "And the hamburgers are out of this world!"

Yummy and Yucky Food

The babies have eaten
some pretty disgusting things:

WORMS
(They called it "chocolate spaghetti.")

SAND
(Phil and Lil used it to make sandwiches.)

CRAYONS
(Chuckie ate two
of Angelica's.)

DOG FOOD

A SPIDER
(Phil)

FOAM FROM SPIKE'S MOUTH

STUFF FROM BELLY BUTTON
(This was Lil's idea.)

LINT FROM POCKETS
(Phil)

GRASSHOPPER JUICE (Lil)

LEAVES
(Chuckie)

But they try NEVER to eat
yucky carrots, peas, or broccoli.

Sniff On, Spike!

Spike loves to sniff around our house and yard. His nose is good for finding things like . . .

Grandpa's room

Buried bones

Burned hamburgers

Old Milk

Spilled Food

Hubert the Garbage Truck Monster

Fire Hydrants

Dirty Shoes

Wet Squirrels

And . . . US!

Joke Break

What kind of storm did Chuckie get caught in?

A worrycane.

Why did Tommy pretend to cry?

He wanted to play bawl.

What does Angelica think the magic words are?

"Tease" and "prank you."

Knock knock?

Who's there?

Kook

Kook who?

Yes, you certainly are.

How does Angelica ask for a tissue?

"Pretty sneeze with booger on top?"

Is it true that Tommy isn't really bald?

No, that's just hairsay.

Why did Tommy leave his crib after dark?

He wanted to be a night crawler.

Where does Angelica get ideas for new pranks?

In the tricktionary.

What did Lil say when she saw Phil's missing button?

"Did sew!"

What did Phil say when he saw Lil's tangled shoelace?

"Did knot!"

Being Rugrats!

THE FIVE WORST THINGS:

- Always being locked in the playpen
- Not being able to drive
- Having a stinky diaper and no one noticing
- Not being able to reach the cookies on the kitchen counter
- Angelica

THE FIVE BEST THINGS:

- Being able to easily crawl under furniture
- Riding Spike
- Small enough to sit on mom's and dad's laps
- No homework
- Everything's an adventure!

What'd They Say?

The little sprouts say the darnedest things! I can't understand 'em half the time, so I made up this handy list to figure it all out!

"Hip-ups" = hiccups

As in, "Those hip-ups are really starting to bug me."

"Pregnuts" = pregnant

As in, "She thought she had the pregnuts."

"Prettyful" = pretty

As in, "Well, she's a girl, like me, so we know she'll be prettyful."

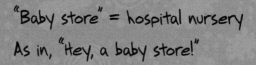

"Baby store" = hospital nursery

As in, "Hey, a baby store!"

"There'll be Nell to pay" = there'll be—oh, never mind . . .

As in, "All I can say is, if they spend all their time takin' care of that Dil and lose Cynthia, there'll be Nell to pay."

"Balsa larm" = false alarm

As in, "My Daddy said it was just a balsa larm."

"Butthound" = bloodhound

As in, "They took Cynthia, Spike! C'mon, you're gonna be my butthound."

"Juice bumps" = goosebumps

As in, "Yeah, this place gives me juice bumps."

"Back to Norman" = back to normal

As in, "Alls we gots to do is knock on his door and say we wanna go home, see, and everything will be back to Norman."